Granny Can't Remember Me
A Children's Book About Alzheimer's

Susan McCormick

Illustrations by Timur Deberdeev

CARROLL PRESS

To—My mom and my boys, whom she loved

Granny Can't Remember Me: A Children's Book About Alzheimer's
Published by Carroll Press
Copyright © 2018 by Susan McCormick

Library of Congress Control Number: 2018949278
ISBN: 978-0-9986187-0-8
Printed in the United States of America

My name is Joey. I am six years old. I have two grandmas.
One is Granny Josie. One is just Granny.

Granny Josie lives in Florida. We take an airplane ride to get to her house. She has a big yard with a garden and flowers that aren't for picking. She swims every day in a pool just for grownups. She has a cookie jar with oatmeal cookies with raisins. I pick out the raisins.

My other Granny lives two blocks away. We walk to get to her house. Only she doesn't live in a house. She lives in a building with a special lock on the inside. Mom calls this safe. Mom says Granny might wander outside and get lost. I once wandered outside and got lost.

Granny loses everything. She loses her glasses. She loses the pictures I draw of whales and penguins. She loses her car keys. Mom says the keys are in a good, safe place. She says the same thing about my pocket knife from Uncle Jim.

Granny likes to talk about her dog, Pickle. He is big, bigger than me, she says. He is a good swimmer, just like me. He loves to play with balls. I love to play with balls. "You'll like Pickle," Granny says. But Granny had Pickle before I was born. I don't tell this to Granny.

Granny can't remember me. She doesn't know my name. She can't remember I like soccer and rockets and dogs, and that I don't like raisins.

I lost my tooth. I scraped my knee. I kicked a goal. But Granny doesn't know.

Mom says Granny used to know everything about everything. Now Granny forgets what she ate for lunch, even if it's macaroni and cheese. So I don't ask. Sometimes Granny forgets to smile. Mom says she is still smiling on the inside. Mom says I should tell Granny everything, even if she can't remember and even if she doesn't smile.

What Granny can remember is stories from the past. She remembers Mom and Uncle Jim when they were little. She tells me Mom cut Uncle Jim's hair playing barber shop. She tells me they played catch with rocks and Uncle Jim got a bump on his head. She tells me Mom hid her green beans in her napkin. She tells me Mom didn't like raisins.

I love Granny's stories. Granny doesn't mind telling them over and over. Granny tells me about when she was a girl. She didn't have any brothers or sisters. I don't have any brothers or sisters. She liked jump rope and Crazy Eights and jacks. I like jump rope and Crazy Eights and jacks.

Sometimes Granny and I play Crazy Eights. Granny can't remember eights are crazy, so I always win.

Mom brings in picture albums for Granny and me. Granny shows me a picture of Mom when she was six, with her hair in two braids. She shows me Uncle Jim with a bow and arrow and no front teeth. She shows me Mom in a hammock reading a book.

Granny shows me a picture of Mom and Dad when they got married. Dad has more hair and Mom isn't wearing glasses. She shows me their first house and their first dog. She doesn't understand when I tell her he's my dog, too.

Granny's favorite story is her Three Best Days. It's my favorite story, too. Granny has three pictures by her bed that are her Three Best Days. One is a picture of Granny holding Mom when she was a baby. That was Best Day Number One. One is a picture of Granny and Uncle Jim when he was tiny. Best Day Number Two.

Granny reaches out and puts her finger on the third picture. The third picture is her Very Best Day of All. She says her Very Best Day of All was the day this little boy was born. I smile and give Granny a big hug. Granny doesn't know that little boy is me. But I do.

Granny can't remember me. But Granny loves me. And I love Granny.

About the Author:

Susan McCormick is a doctor who lives in Seattle. She graduated from Smith College and George Washington University Medical School. She is married and has two boys. Her mother and father-in-law had Alzheimer's disease.

About the Illustrator:

Timur Deberdeev is a multi-talented artist living in Uzbekistan.
Thanks also to Chelsea Johnson, who inspired some of these drawings.

About Alzheimer's Disease:

Alzheimer's disease is a brain disorder which largely affects older adults and is the most common cause of memory loss and dementia. There are other kinds of memory loss as well, and all lead to confusion, disorientation and frustration. Dementia affects not only memory, but also thinking and behavior. Short term memory loss occurs initially, allowing the person with Alzheimer's to remember events and people from the past much more easily than recent experiences. Symptoms slowly worsen over time.

The cause of Alzheimer's disease is currently unknown. Over 5 million Americans have Alzheimer's disease, and that number will grow quickly as the population ages. Alzheimer's disease is the 6th leading cause of death in the United States.

Currently there is no cure for Alzheimer's disease, but treatment can slow the progression of symptoms. There are many ways to lessen the anxiety of the person with Alzheimer's disease. Avoid asking questions, as even simple questions like what someone had for lunch can provoke confusion and worry when they cannot remember. Instead, say, "It looks like you had macaroni and cheese for lunch. I like macaroni and cheese." Avoid corrections or argument, instead go along with the person whatever their current reality. If they say they need to wait for Jim to arrive before eating, and Jim moved away years ago, say, "He called and said he would be late and for us to start without him."

Tips on caring for someone with Alzheimer's can be found at these websites:

Alzheimer's Association   www.alz.org
Alzheimer's Foundation of America   www.alzfnd.org